D1310391

Stories to Grow By

No Fair!

A Tale in Which Monty Learns Contentment

by Alan Kieda
illustrated by Darcy Bell-Myers

In Celebration™, Grand Rapids, MI

Walnut Hill
Church Library
Bethel, CT 06801

Library of Congress Cataloging-in-Publication Data

Kieda, Alan, 1954-
    No fair! : a tale in which Monty learns contentment / by Alan Kieda ; illustrated by
Darcy Bell-Myers.
        p. cm. -- (Stories to grow by)
    Summary: When Monty the chipmunk makes two new friends who live in a big, fancy
house and have backpacks for collecting nuts, he feels less satisfied with the cozy home
he used to love. Includes Bible verses and facts about chipmunks.
    ISBN 1-56822-596-2 (hardcover)
    [1. Chipmunks--Fiction. 2. Contentment--Fiction. 3. Envy--Fiction. 4. Christian
life--Fiction.] I. Myers, Darcy, ill. II. Title. III. Series.

PZ7.K5344 No 2000
[E]--dc21
                                                                              00-022233

Credits
Author: Alan Kieda
Cover and Inside Illustrations: Darcy Bell-Myers
Project Director/Editor: Alyson Kieda
Editor: Kathryn Wheeler

ISBN: 1-56822-596-2
No Fair!
Copyright © 1999 by In Celebration®
a division of Instructional Fair Group, Inc.
a Tribune Education Company
3195 Wilson Drive NW
Grand Rapids, Michigan 49544

All rights reserved. No part of this publication may be reproduced, stored in a retrieval
system, or transmitted, in any form or by any means, electronic, mechanical, photocopying,
recording, or otherwise, without the prior written permission of the publisher.

For information regarding permission write to:
In Celebration®, P.O. Box 1650, Grand Rapids, MI 49501.

Printed in Singapore

Walnut Hill
Church Library
Bethel, CT 06801

Note to Parents

Exodus 20:17—*"You shall not covet your neighbor's house...or anything that belongs to your neighbor."*

Matthew 6:19-21—*"Do not store up for yourselves treasures on earth,...But store up for yourselves treasures in heaven....For where your treasure is, there your heart will be also."*

God tells us to be happy with what we have, for our real treasures are to be stored in heaven. In this materialistic age, however, it is easy to fall into the trap of comparing ourselves and what we have to others. This children's story prompts us to think twice about playing the comparison game.

Before reading the story: Read the verses above. Ask your children to keep them in mind as you read the story. Discuss jealousy. Are you ever jealous? Of what? Have the children look for ways in which Monty showed jealousy.

After reading the story: Discuss the story. Why was Monty so jealous? What did he learn from his opossum friend? Discuss how contentment is the opposite of jealousy. What treasures do we store in heaven?

Monty Chipmunk was always in a hurry. Every morning, he hurried out to look for berries, nuts, and other treats. All day, he hurried back and forth, carrying these treasures to his home in a hollowed-out tree. "Hurry, hurry, hurry!" he whispered as he rushed out for a berry or an acorn. "Hurry, hurry, hurry!" he exclaimed as he dashed back home...only, with his cheek pouches stuffed with food, it sounded more like "Mrmphy, mrmphy, mrmphy!"

5

Even though he was on the run all day, Monty was a very happy chipmunk. He chirped and clicked with glee when he found a whole walnut or a gleaming raspberry. Each time he saw his cozy little home, he thought, "I'm the luckiest chipmunk alive!"

One afternoon as Monty darted to the stream for a quick sip of water, he saw two chipmunks on the bank. He jumped straight into the air and landed in frozen silence. These chipmunks were different. They had striped packs on their backs!

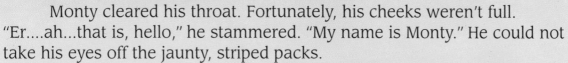

Monty cleared his throat. Fortunately, his cheeks weren't full. "Er....ah...that is, hello," he stammered. "My name is Monty." He could not take his eyes off the jaunty, striped packs.

"I'm Snip," said one of the new chipmunks. "He's Snap. We moved here a few weeks ago. We just came out to fill up our backpacks."

Walnut Hill
Church Library
Bethel, CT 06801

7

"Backpacks?" Monty hesitated over the strange word.

"Yes," said Snap proudly. He spun around to show off the pack. "Aren't they great? So handy!"

"We can carry three times as much as we could in our cheek pouches," said Snip smugly. "And we can talk at the same time! We don't know how we lived without them!"

Monty thought of how he hurried all day to gather food. He felt a heavy weight inside. Monty didn't realize that he was jealous...all he knew was that, suddenly, he didn't feel very good.

Snip and Snap didn't seem to notice as Monty's tail drooped. "We only have to work in the mornings," chattered Snap. "Then we relax in our brand new home."

"Where do you live?" asked Monty.

"Why, Chip Haven, of course! The finest neighborhood. The most spacious burrows. Right next to the stream. We simply wouldn't live anywhere else!" said Snip.

"And our house is the best in the whole neighborhood," added Snap.

"Of course!" agreed Snip.

Monty felt his head spin. "I thought my house was the best place to live!" he thought to himself. "I thought I was the luckiest chipmunk alive! Could it be I've been wrong all this time?"

Through
his confusion, Monty
realized that Snip and
Snap were inviting him to
see their house. Monty stumbled
after them as the two pranced
up the bank. They led Monty to a
maze of roots and tunnels. They
showed him into a magnificent
burrow with arched ceilings of
knotted tree roots. There was room
after room of luxurious storage space.
"Big enough to hold three winters'
worth of food!" said Snap proudly. "And
just look at those shelves! Solid oak!"

"Oak," Monty echoed. "Very nice."
He thought of his little pantry with its
messy, stuffed shelves.

10

"Notice the airy hallways!" said Snip. "So important for keeping food fresh and dry!"

Monty thought of his hollow-tree home. It didn't have a single hallway. Suddenly it seemed stuffy and cramped.

"So, how do you like it?" asked Snip.

"It's okay." Monty choked out the words. He felt awful.

11

That evening, Monty's heart didn't lift when he saw his little house. Instead, the weight inside him got heavier. "It's not fair!" he thought. "Why is my house so far from the stream? Why do I have to make so many trips to get food? And why don't I have a backpack?"

The next morning, Monty didn't scurry and hurry out at sunrise. Instead, he climbed slowly down his tree feeling crabby and tired. When he stuffed a berry in his cheek pouch, he remembered the backpacks. "No fair!" he thought. When he ran across the forest for a drink of water, he thought of Chip Haven, nestled by the stream. "No fair!" he cried. Every time he thought of Snip and Snap, Monty moved more slowly.

One day when Monty was dragging himself to the raspberry bushes, he heard a voice whisper, "Is that you, Monty?" A pink nose poked its way through a leafy bush. The whiskers quivered. It was Monty's opossum friend, Portnoy.

"It's me," said Monty miserably.

"I've never seen you like this," said Portnoy. "What's the problem?"

At first, the heavy weight inside Monty made it hard for him to talk, but suddenly, the words rushed out. "Chip Haven...hallways... afternoons off...oak shelves... backpacks!"

Portnoy listened quietly. He nodded. After Monty described the backpacks for the third time, Portnoy said, "You know, Monty, when I was a young opossum, I was very jealous of an opossum who was bigger and stronger than I was. He seemed to have everything. The more I wished I was him, the more miserable I became."

"What happened?" asked Monty.

"Well, one morning a bobcat came through the forest. The other opossum and I played dead, of course, but the other opossum's nose twitched. The bobcat leaped toward him. So I quickly rolled down a hill to confuse the bobcat. It kept him from carrying the other opossum away.

"Later, I found out that that other opossum envied me for being so clever! And that's when I began to realize that I had gifts of my own. I started to count my blessings."

"Count my blessings," Monty echoed. He thought about those words all the way home. The next morning, he went out early to find food.

"Count my blessings, count my blessings," he muttered.

15

As Monty scurried back and forth he thought, "Well, I have Portnoy.
He's a good friend." Monty felt a little happier. "I have plenty of food, even
though I don't have oak shelves," he thought. He began to scurry faster. "And
I know the best raspberry patch in the forest!" he shouted. "And I can run
faster than any chipmunk I know!" It began to drizzle. "And I love the rain!"
Monty raced back toward his little house. His heart felt light again.

By the time Monty got home, the gentle drizzle had turned into a downpour. "I'm thankful for raspberry crumble for dinner," he said. "I'm thankful for a cozy bed to sleep in when it storms!"

It rained for days. Monty kept busy by taking inventory of his pantry. Then he started to build a little set of shelves. "Hurry, hurry, hurry," he hummed as he hammered.

On the sixth day of the storm, there was a knock on his door. On the welcome mat stood two shivering chipmunks. They tumbled into his parlor.

"Snip and Snap!" said Monty. "What are you doing here?"

"S-s-sorry to barge in," chattered Snap, "b-but we're f-f-freezing!"

"The stream overflowed into our house," said Snip. "All our storerooms are under water! C-c-could we stay with you for a few days?"

"That's a great idea. We can get to know each other," said Monty cheerfully.

As Snip dried off, Snap looked around. "We are so thankful you have this cozy little house!" he said.

"You know what?" Monty answered. "So am I!"

A Note About Chipmunks

The chipmunk is the lively, chattering relative of the squirrel. Chipmunks look like squirrels but are smaller and have striped backs.

Chipmunks are found in Asia and North America. Most American chipmunks are about 8 inches (20 cm) long from head to tip of tail.

Chipmunks live in burrows dug under rocks or tree roots or in old logs. Their burrows contain storerooms and leaf-lined nests. Chipmunks eat nuts, seeds, wild fruits, and berries. They have inner cheek pouches which they can stuff with food. When their pouches are full, chipmunks scurry to their burrows to deposit their food. Chipmunks sleep through much of the winter but may awaken on warm winter days to eat.

Chipmunks are fairly skilled at climbing and swimming.